This book is dedicated to my loving husband, who convinced me to write.

Acknowledgements:

So many amazing and wonderful people have gone into this project, far too many to name individually, so I'll just lump you all into the same group. What could possibly go wrong?

To my family, all of my family from coast to coast and around the world, for supporting me and uplifting me.

To my friends, for encouraging me and putting up with me.

To my church family, for listening.

To you, for reading.

Thank you all, from the bottom of my heart.

CAPTAIN GRANT MASON

Vs

THE BLACK TALONS

Rebecca M. Norris

www.rebeccanorrisbooks.com

Duskraven Entertainment, LLC

For more information about Rebecca M. Norris, visit rebeccanorrisbooks.com.

Paperback ISBN: 979-8-9850971-0-8

Library of Congress Control Number: 2021920871

Printed in the USA.

Duskraven Entertainment, LLC
PO Box 3795
Olathe, KS 66063

Cover Design: Rebecca M. Norris
Editor: Scott Norris

IMPERIAL N'KAHVIAN FLEET

ಬ 1 ಛ

Capt. Grant Mason of the O.N.S. T'Naan grunted as he lifted the scaffolding from the entrance to the maintenance tube on deck five. Why *he* was the one lifting the scaffolding when he had a crew of other people was beyond him. Where were they anyway? His engineer should be doing this. He had discovered a compression gradient in the atomic power core while manning the conn. If he didn't get it fixed soon the entire coupling would destabilize and that would cost him valuable time and resources to replace. Not to mention the potential to completely destroy his ship... again. It was *atomic* after all. He had... damaged... (dented, more like dented)... three frigates already and didn't really want to replace this one. He'd taken a liking to the T'Naan. She had a soul, this ship did. Much more than any other A.I. controlled vessel. A spirit. A fire that he appreciated. Especially in his line of work. He was a merchant for the Imperial N'Kahvian Fleet, and the N'Kahv Empire was *the* ruling force in this half of the galaxy. He needed their resources and influence to maneuver in the Black Market deals that he sometimes undertook. Having a ship that could turn on a *h'nta* was always a plus! Hasty escapes were a fact of life! Right now, they were on their way to... acquire, yeah... some military grade magnatomic particle dispersers that the Order of the Dauntless desperately needed in their fight against K'Lon, the ruling force in the *other* half of the galaxy.

See, the Imperial N'Kahvian Fleet has three main divisions; his, which was the merchant branch named the Order of the Night Shade; the diplomatic corps, the Order of the Morning Light; and the military branch, the Order of the Dauntless. Sometimes the First Kahv, the highest N'Kahvian ruler, would authorize special missions for the merchant branch, like now, when resources were spread thin for one of the other two. As a merchant, he and the other captains had ties to the Black Market Conglomerate, neutral "third party vendors" in the conflict between N'Kahv and K'Lon. The problem is that the Black Market has no leader. None whatsoever. Each... vendor... is affiliated with one of three main powers; the Black Talons – with whom he was on his way to meet – the Silver Daggers, and the Red Moons. The Talons were the meanest of the lot, but they also had the best weapons and tech. The Daggers specialized in assassination and espionage, and the Moons preferred to broker information in exchange for currency, weapons, and tech in the

Black Eye Galaxy, what the Terrans referred to as NGC 4826.

In fact, Grant Mason was the last Terran in this galaxy. They pulled out about 135 years ago when their entire meta-warp network collapsed. Several billion Terrans were trapped in various parts of the Virgo Supercluster, never to return home again. Mason's parents were among them. He was just a kid when it all happened, but he remembers the anxiety and panic on their faces when they realized their Alcubierre Drive went inoperable, unable to connect to the relays. They decided to take the long nap of cryo-sleep and set the ship on autopilot to the nearest galaxy, NGC 4826. When they arrived 30 years ago, and the A.I. brought everyone out of stasis, they were immediately attacked and apprehended by the K'Lonians. Long story short, the N'Kahvians rescued them but his parents died of their wounds while in transit to the capitol. He was raised by the head of the Order of the Night Shade and has worked for them ever since. The Terrans? No one knows.

He liked his job. It paid well, gave him a measure of respect in the community, and most importantly, it let him fly! Except, of course, in times like this where there was a malfunction and he couldn't locate his crew…

"T'Naan, have you located *any* member of my crew yet? I really shouldn't be the one down here and leaving no one on the bridge to take care of things…"

"Sorry, Cap. What was that? I was busy flying the ship, plotting navigational course corrections, and slowing the destabilization of the power couplings," she said with sarcasm dripping from her voice.

"I apologize. I know you can handle things perfectly fine without all us mortals getting in the way. It's just... I want to be on the bridge! Where's Xhuvina, anyway? She should be the one down here..."

"Engineer Xhuvina is in the mess hall."

"The mess hall? Why is she there? She doesn't even eat!"

"Correction, Cap. Tukkols do eat; they just don't eat the same things you fleshy, carbon-based types do. She maintains a regular diet of limestone and shale. Sometimes, she throws in a little nutrient-enhanced soil, too."

"Stop getting mouthy with me, T'Naan," Mason crawled further into the maintenance tube and turned left into the hatchway for the power core. From there he could access the coupling that was experiencing problems and hopefully fix it. Things were getting pretty hot, he'd better hurry.

"Alright then, where is Rhiv? Maybe he can come fix this."

"Operations Officer Rhivakkon is in the mess hall."

"Again with the mess hall... What about J'Sepp, Kotzer, Laylaka, or Bellatan. Are they *all* in the mess hall?"

"Yep! Sure are!" T'Naan said. "By the way, you might want to hurry. Core temperatures have just exceeded 400 Kelvin. Maybe you should wear a suit, huh?"

"What?!" Mason quickly backed away from the interior

hatch to the core. He needed Xhuvina down here. Being a silicon-based Tukkol she could withstand temperatures up to 800 Kelvin.

"Page Xhuvina! Get her down here, now!"

"Sure, no need to yell at me..." Was it Mason's imagination or did the *ship* actually sound *hurt*?! AI's were strange creations...

Within moments he heard the thunderous sound of Xhuvina rolling down the corridor. Her massive form closely resembled piles of solid rock, melted and hardened into a smooth sheen, and virtually impenetrable. People generally steered clear of Tukkols but once they got to know Xhuvina they realized there would never be a truer, more valued friend in all the universe. He didn't know why she chose to be an engineer instead of security, like most of her kind. It must be very difficult to handle the delicate controls and intricate webbing of a starship without true fingers, but she was the best in the business. He asked for her personally when he was given his first frigate, the T'Kela, and they have been together ever since.

"What's up, Cap?" Xhuvina asked as she hit a few buttons on the wall terminal. "Ah, never mind. I'll fix this in no time!" She opened a panel in the wall, hit a few more buttons and closed it again.

"There! All done!"

Mason was floored. "You mean, all I had to do was hit some *buttons*!? I nearly baked myself trying to get into the hatch!"

"Why'd you do that, Cap? It's hot in there." Xhuvina said

as she turned around and went back down the hall towards the lift. "You coming?"

Mason just shook his head and followed after her. That Tukkol never ceased to amaze him and she *was* the best in the business... but still... the ship could have *exploded*!

"All you had to do was purge the plasma from the injector relays, and then flush the core with coolant." Xhuvina turned to face him; her steel colored eyes were more piercing than others of her race. Mason had a hard time holding her gaze and looked away. "You could have done that from the bridge. No need to come down here."

"T'Naan, you could have mentioned that. Why didn't *you* just take care of it?" Mason inquired.

"You didn't ask, Cap." He just shook his head again. He should learn to stop asking these questions.

He'd only been with this crew for six months and only two of them came with him from his previous ships, Xhuvina, and his best friend and first officer, Bellatan. T'Naan was an enigma at the best of times, but they got along well, and she did try to help him out from time to time. Even so, Mason was always shaking his head at one or another of his crew. Like now, why were they *all* in the mess hall? Didn't anyone care that they were about to enter Talon territory? He pondered these and other questions as he walked into the mess hall on deck three.

"Surprise! Happy birthday!" Cheers erupted from the six other people onboard the small ship. Well, seven if Mason included T'Naan. Her sultry voice was unmistakable in the midst of the others. He had completely forgotten that today was his 35th birthday. Rather easy to forget since N'Kahvians didn't celebrate birthdays and the Terran calendar was unfamiliar to the other races. He usually just skipped this day altogether, but it seemed that this crew wasn't going to let it pass unnoticed.

"What? Uh… thanks!" Mason looked around at the faces gathered in the mess for his benefit. Xhuvina was just to his left, giddy and grinning like a school girl. Bell was there, too, on his right. Not only was he the first officer, but he also doubled as Mason's science officer. His race closely resembled Terrans, but with some differences. Ahmbians had reptilian eyes with dual lids, their knees bent the opposite direction from Terrans, and they had virtually no nose or olfactory glands. Mason tried to describe the scent of his favorite food to him once, but that was like trying to describe color to a man with no eyes. Bell simply didn't understand how wonderful spaghetti could be! Not for the first time Mason wondered why he decided to make Bell the ship's cook…

Next to Bellatan was the ship's medical officer, a N'Kahvian named J'Sepp. J'Sepp was typical of his race, insectoid. A bipedal with green chitin for skin, four arms with four fingers each, black eyes and a scratchy voice. N'Kahvians were impervious to disease and most ended up in the medical field. A typical N'Kahvian merchant ship had two N'Kahvians on board but since Mason was practically born and raised on N'Kahv they considered him one of their own. Talk about an interesting childhood! But that was another story.

Next to J'Sepp stood the most incredibly beautiful creature Mason had ever seen, Laylaka. She was the ship's navigational officer. Since Rusali females were considered extremely attractive to other races very few ever left the homeworld unless it was to join the Morning Light – beauty has its advantages when negotiating the release of hostages, after all. Laylaka was among the most beautiful and had been Mason's crush since she came on board. They met by accident while Mason was on a mission to the Daggers base in the Azlan sector. She was being chased by some… men… of ill-repute and ran into him at full speed. All Mason saw was a flash of orange before he hit the ground, on top of her. He quickly got up and reached down to help her when he got his first full glimpse of her. She had orange skin, green eyes, no hair, very little clothing, and all the right curves. He was in love. She begged him to take her aboard ship, promised to be the best navigation officer he'd ever seen, and lived up to her promise.

Next to her was Kotzer, his head of security and weapons officer. Brokering this deal with the Talons was going to fall to him since he could tell a bad disperser from a good one, something Mason didn't have a clue about and didn't want one either. Kotzer was another Ahmbian. He stood about a head taller than Mason, and was twice as muscular as a male Rusali! He didn't know much else about Kotzer, but he knew he could rely on him to protect the ship and crew, and he was a stickler for protocol. They had seen their share of skirmishes already and Kotzer always came through.

That brought Mason back around to his side of the room where Rhivakkon was standing, next to Xhuvina. Rhiv was a Myowan, a long lived, cat-like race that was fairly new to intergalactic commerce. In fact, they looked exactly like cats but they stood on two legs, lived for 500 years, and spoke eloquently. Mason enjoyed the deeply rolled 'R's' that Myowans were notorious for using. Rhiv was also the best operations officer he had ever had the pleasure of working with. He knew each class of ship intimately and all of the peculiarities of the T'Naan. He was incredibly brilliant and could always get them out of tight situations with his ingenuity. Mason also suspected Rhiv was in love with Xhuvina. He was never far from her side.

Yes, even though he didn't understand his crew all the time, he knew he could count on them. And they had planned a birthday party for him. *Could this day get any better?* He smiled and walked further into the room.

"I was wondering what everyone was doing in the mess instead of at their posts. Was that whole power core thing a setup to get me off the bridge?"

"Yep! Sure was!" T'Naan said. "Don't worry; I wouldn't have let you blow me up. I kinda like living, you know. But we couldn't think of any other way of getting you out of that chair! We didn't count on you trying to fix it yourself, though. That was just foolish."

"Indeed! You could have been hurt! Do you know how much trouble it would be to find a new captain this late in the mission?" Laylaka said and winked. She came over to his side and placed a kind of wreath of interwoven vines and leaves on his head and then draped the long tail of it over his shoulder. "This is a traditional Life Day crown among Rusali. We give this to each person on their Life Day, what you call birthday, to honor them and show them respect. It means that they have succeeded in surviving the harsh realities of this universe for another year. Each year we add a new section to the wreath. You have 35 sections! Something to be celebrated!" She had the most beautiful, musical accent, sort of a cross between his Russian mother's voice and his Italian father's voice. It brought back fond memories and made her so much more enticing... Mason could forgive her for hinting at getting a new captain, just this once. Who was he kidding; he could never blame her for anything! And orange was his new favorite color.

"Bell to Mase! Bell to Mase! Come in Captain Mason!" Bell was tapping Mason on the head repeatedly. "Stop mooning over Laylaka and come cut your cake!" Everyone laughed. Did they *all* know he was in love with Laylaka? Did *Laylaka* know!? As Mason looked around he knew it was true. *Could this day get any worse?*

୫୦ 2 ଓଷ

This is the worst day ever! Mason thought as he banked hard to port to evade weapons fire. The disaster at the birthday celebration ended with Laylaka giving him a sympathy peck on the cheek. The cake was horrible and smelled like rotten eggs – which is precisely what it was made with. *Never trust a man with no nose to make your birthday cake,* he thought. The gift that the crew bought him would have been nice if he wasn't deathly allergic to *k'ntaka* fur. *Good thing the doc was there...* And to top it all off, the Talons were firing on them for no reason whatsoever! *Well, ok, I guess maybe ignoring their hails was a bad idea, but no one was on the bridge and T'Naan didn't think it was the right time to mention it. I need to have a serious talk with her... if we get out of this alive, that is...* He banked hard to starboard to avoid another volley. Laylaka was calculating escape routes rapidly while keeping the crew aware of hazards in their path. They were about to make her job harder by entering an asteroid belt. Mason hoped the T'Naan was agile enough to maneuver in there because they were out of options.

"Heading 134 mark 296, Captain! I can plot a course through the field but we must enter *at that point*!" Laylaka shouted and grabbed the edge of her console as the ship reeled from plasma cannon fire.

Yep, the Talons sure do have the best weapons… wish we weren't on this *side of 'em, though!* Mason was having a hard time at conn. Listening to Laylaka's shouted directions, ordering return fire, hollering for engineering to give him more power to the engines, and fighting the leafy monstrosity that was still on his head was exhausting! He almost fell out of his seat as yet another volley of cannon fire assaulted them.

"Rhiv, try hailing them again!" Mason called as he entered in another set of evasion commands.

"Yes, sirrr!" He tapped a few buttons and then yelled, "They arrre rrresponding!"

"This is Captain Crayvorn of the Black Talons. Why have you entered our space and ignored our hails?"

"I'm Captain Grant Mason of the O.N.S. T'Naan. We are here to negotiate a trade agreement with Mak D'Neen. I'm sorry we didn't answer your hails; no one was available at the time. We… had something come up." Another plasma cannon round blasted the ship. The shields couldn't take much more of it.

"Please stop trying to kill us so we can talk. The cannon fire is really making this difficult."

Captain Crayvorn called an order to someone off to the side, and then pulled out his own magnatomic particle disperser. There was a flash of yellow-blue light and then all was silent.

"There, is that better?" Capt. Crayvorn said.

"Uh... yeah, thanks, I guess... All stop." *Who am I dealing with here?!?* As the ship came to a full stop just outside the asteroid belt he canceled the alert status onboard the ship, but kept what was left of the shields up. *Just in case he wants to try that whole blasting-us-out-of-the-sky thing again...*

"You will remain where you are. We will tow your ship. Try anything and I will not hesitate to destroy you. Is that understood, *Captain* Mason?" The contempt oozed from him like the slime on Ahmbia 3.

"Yeah, sure, no problem. All you had to do was ask." Mason fidgeted in his seat. No one gave orders to him, but then again, Crayvorn was the one pointing two plasma cannons at him. Mason decided maybe this time he would just follow the order. Safer that way, right?

"We did." Crayvorn cut the transmission and the ship jolted as the tritonic energy beam took hold to tow them along like *g'thanes* on a leash. *How humiliating. This day couldn't possibly get any worse...*

At some point in the near future – he hoped – he would

learn to stop saying that, because, despite all the odds, his day really could get worse. He was discovering that now…

Captain Crayvorn herded, yes *herded*, them all to the main Talons base in the sector. He had them bound and gagged once he boarded their ship, and then tied them all together on one long rope. Mason took the lead on that rope, followed by his bridge crew, Bellatan, Laylaka, and Rhivakkon. J'Sepp, Xhuvina, and Kotzer, who was manning the weapons array on deck two, followed. Crayvorn paraded, yes *paraded*, them around the main drag and brought them to a dilapidated building at the end of the street. Once inside he removed the bindings and left. That's it, just untied them and left.

Mason had had dealings with the Talons in the past, but it typically went smoother than this. Then again, he had never ignored their hails before. Never fired on them. Didn't sass them. They had the best weapons and tech in the galaxy and he knew it. He also knew what they were capable of *if* they were so inclined. They could easily take over the entire galaxy, everyone knew it, and that's how they kept power. The threat was enough. Right now, he had some of that impressive weaponry trained on him and his crew. The dimly lit room was full of armed guards and mercs just looking for a fight. There was a table in the center with five men of different races playing a card game.

"So… you're Captain Grant Mason, huh?" The one in the blue shirt said. The others laughed.

"Not much to look at, is he boss?" One of the others at the

table said. They were all wearing black jumpsuits with an impossible number of pockets and patches except for the guy in blue. Mason figured he must be the highest ranking Talon here. In the past, he had only dealt with the thugs and maybe one or two of the higher-ups, but they always wore black. It was rumored that the top echelon wore blue dress shirts and black jackets, but he'd never seen anyone. Supposedly, there were only three in the upper echelon, brothers. *What if this is one of them?* Mason thought. No one had ever seen one of The Brothers, so no one knew what they looked like or what race they were. Mason was both intrigued and not a little bit frightened.

"I'm Mike Brantoni, but you can call me sir. Or Mr. Brantoni if it entertains you. It's a pleasure to make your acquaintance, Captain Mason." He stood and offered his hand. Of course, Mason took it. Slowly, so that everyone there knew he was no threat. "My younger brothers and I run the Black Talons. We like to stay in the shadows, but you seem to have stumbled into our nest and killed one of my men. Now what should I do about that...?" He stepped further into the light and Mason gasped. He was Terran!

ଛ 3 ଔ

"Y-you're Terran! You're like me! How?" Mason was shocked, stunned, awed, and not a little bit confused. He truly believed he was the last Terran alive in this galaxy. The N'Kahvians had done a thorough search for anyone else from his race so that he would at least grow up among his own kind. When that failed, they raised him themselves, although they had no idea how to handle a five year old Terran boy.

"Let's just say we're of a kind, you and me." Brantoni took out a small, dried reed from his pocket and lit it. The air instantly filled with sweet smelling smoke, so thick Mason could cut it with a knife. "Now, back to my original question. You came to the wrong part of this sector. What do you think a good businessman, such as myself, should do about that?"

"Oh, I know! Let us go!" Mason nervously chuckled at

what he thought was a very funny joke. Until the back of Brantoni's hand found the most sensitive part of Mason's face. He understood immediately that this was no laughing matter. He needed to control his nerves before he did anything else unbecoming of a starship captain. He spat out the blood that had pooled in his mouth.

"I wanna know why you killed Mak. Tell me that, and maybe I'll let your friends go." Brantoni took another puff of his biri.

"I didn't kill anybody! We just got here!" Mason knew this was serious. What was going on? Was he being framed for something?

"Bruto says you were supposed to meet with Mak. Funny thing is, Mak's dead. Your course took you *right past* his hidey-hole. A little too convenient, don't you think?"

"We didn't have anything to do with that! You must believe us! We just got here!" Laylaka said, imploring Brantoni to listen. One of Brantoni's men grabbed her arm and forced her to kneel.

"You let go of her!" Mason roared and took a swing. He missed of course; he was still woozy from Brantoni's blow. *I should really learn how to fight...* he thought as he spun in a full circle.

"Let her go. We strive to be gentlemen, here, remember?" As soon as Laylaka was clear Brantoni gave a silent signal to one of his guards. The guard pulled out a disperser, set it to low and fired. The man that grabbed Laylaka glowed brightly, screamed violently, and disintegrated slowly.

"That was the lowest setting. Something we save for the lowest kind of scum. As I understand, it's really quite a painful way to die. He deserved no less." Brantoni turned to Laylaka and gently touched her arm. "Are you alright, my dear? I apologize for that. My men... sometimes they come to me without brains. Here, take my chair and sit down. Maz, get the lady a drink." Laylaka shook as she sat down and promptly retched all over the floor. Mason didn't blame her. He was close to doing the same. *He just killed him! Slowly turning his body to dust! The pain he must have felt as he died... We have to get out of here!*

"Maybe we can help you, sir." Mason gingerly felt his way around to Laylaka and rested a hand on her shoulder. She clutched his hand, hard. "You said Mak is dead, but we truly just arrived here. You can check our logs. We haven't stopped since the refueling station on Alterion 7. There's no way we could have killed him. But maybe we can track down who did."

"And what is it you want in return for your... assistance?" Brantoni sat in another chair and puffed.

"Well, we were supposed to purchase some magnatomic particle dispersers from him. Honor his agreement and we're even. Is that acceptable?"

Brantoni puffed and thought. Thought and puffed. "No, it isn't," he said at last. He stood up and walked over to Mason; stood less than two inches from him, and puffed biri smoke into his face.

"You work for me now." With that Brantoni turned and left, one hand in his pocket. Guards came and grabbed each of Mason's people. They were taken to a large, dark room. With finality they heard the door lock.

Someone was crying. Mason couldn't tell who. Someone else was feeling the walls for weak spots. He guessed it was Kotzer. Someone else was humming. He knew it was Xhuvina. She always hummed when she was frightened. She said it calms her and helps her think clearly. Mason joined in and hoped that the act would have the same effect on him. He needed to think his way out of this. He was no fighter, he was a thinker. N'Kahvians, despite their impervious shells, were actually very frail creatures. They fought with their minds not their hands. Intelligence was their strongest asset. That's why they had the Order of the Dauntless which was mostly comprised of Rusali and Tukkols. Those races were much better suited for hand-to-hand, ground, and aerial combat, and Mason had never had the chance to travel to Rusali or Tukkol or even train under a skilled fighter. No, he needed his brains to get everyone out of this safely. *Think, Mase, think...*

As Xhuvina's sorrowful tune filled the air Bellatan called out to him. "Mase, where are ya, buddy?"

"Over here. Just follow my voice. What's on your mind?" Mason asked as Bell sat beside him on the floor. Bell took a long sigh, and Mason knew his best friend well enough to know that he also rested his head in his hands, even though it was pitch black in the room where they were being held and he couldn't see him.

"I've been thinking. I know, I know, dangerous, but really. Why do they think *we* killed Mak D'Neen? We weren't even here. The logs prove we never even went to Mak's base. We had to take that detour around the gravitational eddy, remember? That course correction diverted us by two days and brought us too far outside of Mak's zone. So, why do they think we did this thing? What evidence could they have?"

"That's true. Our course brought us past Byanco 6, nowhere near Mak... So, why..." Mason wished he had T'Naan's database handy. He began to wonder if there was another ship just like his out there. One that was in the sector at the same moment he was. One that, if it truly was a N'Kahvian merchant ship, was now wanted for treason. The delicate balance of power among the N'Kahvians, the K'Lonians, and the Black Market Conglomerate came with rules. No ship, from either the N'Kahvians or the K'Lonians, could attack, disable, or destroy a Black Market ship. Neither could they imprison or execute a member of the Black Market. In return for this protection and freedom to conduct business, the Black Market agreed to disclose any purchases that could potentially annihilate an entire species. No one wanted to be responsible for genocide, after all. They also agreed not to hold any citizen of either governing force without just cause and notification to N'Kahv or K'Lon, in which case the Order of the

Morning Light would step in to negotiate the release. All parties agreed to prominently display their faction colors, emblem, and division on their ships and persons. Each of Mason's crew wore the unmistakable green jumpsuit of the Imperial N'Kahvian Fleet with the seal of the Night Shade embroidered on the left breast, even Xhuvina, whose jumpsuit was specially made for her rolling Tukkol form.

As Mason recalled the specifics of the strange marriage among factions it occurred to him that this could be a plot by K'Lonians to destroy the Accord. Or the Black Market to throw suspicion on K'Lon or N'Kahv. Or the diabolical plot of N'Kahv – scratch that – *someone else* to sever ties and throw the entire galaxy into chaos!

"But they can't do that!" Mason burst out.

"Who can't do what?" Bell said. "Remember, Mase, we're not in that brain of yours with you. What are you thinking? Did you figure this out?"

"Possibly… I need more information first." Mason stood and started to feel the wall in much the same way he supposed Kotzer did. "Kotzer, did you find anything?"

"Over here, sir. There's some sort of indention in the wall here... Only big enough for one person to pass through at a time."

Mason pressed on the indention but it wouldn't budge. "It must be the door we came in by, but there's no handle, no keyhole, no hinges…" Mason stepped back a few feet and gave the door his strongest running kick… which nearly shattered every bone in his body. He landed in a heap on the floor.

"Cap! What possessed you to do that?" Xhuvina ceased her humming and hurried over to him.

"I was trying to get someone's attention. Ohh, ow. Okay, one more time." He stood as if to try again, but Xhuvina beat him to it. She knocked on the door with the power and strength of, well, a Tukkol.

The door opened and a guard yelled, "Stop doing that! You'll wake the dead! Again..." He turned on a handheld beam of light and searched the faces of the people in the room. Finally, he landed on Mason. "You. What is it?"

"I need to see Brantoni, er *Mister* Brantoni, please. It's important!" Mason hobbled over to the beam of light, but the other guard pushed him back. "I think I know what's going on here, but I need to speak with him!"

"Yeah, yeah, alright already. Hold on." The door closed and locked again, but opened a few moments later. "Alright, boss-man will see you now. C'mon."

As Mason stepped out into the dimly lit hallway he finally got a glimpse of the two guards escorting him. One was Tukkol, but the other was Nipoli, a race that sided with K'Lon during the uprising. Nipoli could superheat their skin to the point of intense luminescence. Anyone dumb enough to be touching them at the time would find their hands, or other parts, burned to a crisp! Mason scooted closer to the Tukkol.

Within moments he was back in the same room where he

first met Brantoni. Again, Brantoni was sitting at the table playing cards.

"So, you think you know who killed my man, huh?" Brantoni set down his cards. "Straight flush. I win!"

"Not so fast, boss! I have a *Royal* Flush!!!" One of the men at the table, a Rusali, jumped up and down, cheering.

"No, *you* have a straight flush. *I* have a Royal Flush." Brantoni switched the cards. "The pot is all mine!"

"Boss! I won! That's *my* money!" The Rusali reached for the stack of *h'ngol* bills on the table. Instantly, Brantoni grabbed his hand, wrenched it backwards, threw him against the wall, took out a sidearm, and fired.

"I win. Any more objections?" The other three men at the table merely shook their heads.

"Congratulations, Boss!" They all said in unison.

"Now, Mason. It looks like we have an open seat at the table. How's about you join us and we'll chat." Mason knew better than to argue. He sat in the now vacant seat at the table while its previous occupant still smoked in the corner, nothing more than ash. Brantoni walked over to his former poker buddy and draped a white sheet over the dust. "Courtesy, boys, we must always be gentleman after all." He stood a moment more and then walked over to the table.

"Now then, where were we?" Brantoni smiled and dealt the cards. Mason knew this game, this one game of poker, could cost him his life. He had to play wisely and carefully. He suspected Brantoni would use the game to gauge Mason's character, to assess his honor and integrity, to determine who among his crew should live and who should die. Mason gulped and prepared himself for battle.

ಬಿ 4 ಆ

Mason returned to the holding cell unharmed several cycles later, with orders to seek out Rashal Nalaadi of the Red Moons. Brantoni suspected that someone was framing not only the N'Kahvians, but the Talons as well. Information brokers, such as the Moons, would know who and why. Mason was lucky to have learned how to play Texas Hold 'Em, and was glad that T'Naan enjoyed the game as well. Her love of the game meant that he always had a playing partner. Being an A.I. she could adjust to his skill level and she always kept him challenged. He'd have to remember to treat her to something special when he got back aboard ship.

Once Mason had earned Brantoni's trust through the game, Brantoni shared his suspicions with him. Mak D'Neen was on a secret assignment to meet with Nalaadi and discover who had been sabotaging all of the Talon's shipments to N'Kahv and

K'Lon. Brantoni learned from Mason that *none* of the shipments of weapons had arrived on the N'Kahvian homeworld, even though they had been sent regularly, which was why Mason was assigned to personally bring the weapons home. The First Kahv suspected that the Talons were simply keeping the money and denying the Dauntless the weapons they needed. Now Mason knew otherwise, and Brantoni had another piece of the puzzle. They both suspected the same was happening on the K'Lonian homeworld. But who would want to destroy trade agreements among the three biggest ruling factions in the galaxy? It just didn't make sense. Brantoni decided to seek the aid of Grant Mason, well known for getting out of tough situations using his brain alone; a fact that Brantoni was glad to have witnessed himself.

Brantoni was measuring Mason and indeed his entire crew to see how they would handle the allegation of murder, and the staged attack. If Mason lied and said they *had* murdered him in order to appear stronger, Brantoni would have killed them all. If Mason lied and said they weren't going to meet Mak at all, Brantoni would have killed them all. If Mason tried to manipulate him or seek to alter things to his own advantage in any way, Brantoni would have killed them all. Instead, Mason gathered all the facts that he had access to, evaluated the situation, and concluded that it must be some sort of elaborate setup; a conclusion that Brantoni had already drawn. The fact that Mason figured it out in less than ten cycles when it took him weeks just proved Brantoni had made the right choice. When Mak was found dead soon after learning the truth Brantoni had to speed up his timeline. There was no record of what Mak found, no evidence, not even a recording as to what happened. Brantoni needed answers. So did Mason. So did N'Kahv. So did K'Lon.

But nobody really cares about K'Lon anyway… Mason thought as he decided how much of this information to reveal to his crew and how much was best kept secret. *What we need to do now is get back aboard the T'Naan and retrace Mak's steps, see if we can find this Rashal Nalaadi fellow, and solve the biggest conspiracy since the Uprising! No problem.*

Mason filled his crew in on the basics and soon they were released and back aboard the T'Naan. Their first stop was to locate Mak's base about 300 parsecs from Brantoni's hideout. As they were en route J'Sepp called Mason down to the med bay on deck four.

"Now, Grant," J'Sepp started. He was really the only one that ever used Mason's first name. Usually people just called him Mason, or Cap. He was still getting used to it, but the old N'Kahvian reminded him of his adopted grandfather, so Mason humored him. "Why are you helping the Talons in this way? What is really happening here? I know you well enough to know when you are not telling us everything. This is a small ship and we need to be able to rely on each other, moment by moment. We should not do this. We should report back to the First Khav and let the Dauntless handle these types of missions. Tracking down a murderer? We are not suited for such things."

They were secure in the med bay, but J'Sepp still switched to the N'Kahvian tongue. The other races had a *very* difficult time pronouncing the strange clipped tones the N'Kahvian and K'Lonian languages contained, so the common tongue in the galaxy was that of the Ahmbians; easy to learn with very little in the way of linguistic nuances. Mason knew there must be a lot on J'Sepp's mind to use his native language.

"T'Naan, security override on this room only. No recording or monitoring, please."

"Sure Cap, but do you promise to tell me later?"

"T'Naan."

"Sorry, Cap. Going silent. Nothing inside this room will be recorded, monitored, or eavesdropped. Promise." There was a slight click when a very dejected T'Naan shut off the monitors.

"It's like this, Doc," Mason started in the N'Kahvian tongue, just in case one of the others could still listen in. "We stumbled into something huge! Something that could destroy the very fabric of this galaxy. This mission requires a delicate touch and near-complete anonymity. Yes, we are tracking a murderer, but it's more than that. Maybe you should sit down."

"I thought as much. Please, continue." J'Sepp sat on one of the beds in what could be mistaken for Indian style if they were back on Terra.

"Mak D'Neen was on special assignment to track down the missing shipments of weapons and goods to *both* militaries. But it went deeper than that. Brantoni suspects that the shipments were not sabotaged, but diverted, to some third party. Mak was killed while in possession of the truth. We have the ability to travel this sector of space without suspicion. A military ship would be flagged and followed immediately. That's why Brantoni chose us. Furthermore, this third party is using N'Kahvian ships! I don't have to tell you what that would mean, do I?"

"Indeed not," J'Sepp was stunned. "If this is true, then not only would N'Kahv be guilty of breaking the Accord that has lasted since the Uprising, but we would have the Black Market Conglomerate, the Republic of Free K'Lon, and all of the military forces in this galaxy on our doorstep in mere moments. This could start a war far bigger, far greater, and far more deadly than the Uprising ever was! Tell me that N'Kahv has not done this thing!"

"Well, I don't know, J'Sepp, but I'm going to find out. I believe, as does Brantoni, that N'Kahv is being set up to take the fall for this, and that the Black Talons are taking the fall within the Conglomerate. See, we have pieced together that by sabotaging the military shipments to *both* sides while using N'Kahvian ships the K'Lonians would have no choice but to assume that we hijacked our own ships to divert suspicion while destroying their means of fighting back. The Talons would also be caught in a conundrum. If they continue to supply weapons and armor, knowing that the ships are being attacked, then they are guilty of subverting the K'Lonian war effort, but if they withhold the shipments they are guilty of aiding the enemy and breaking the Accord. The Daggers and the Moons would wipe them out, superior firepower notwithstanding. Don't forget, the Black Market can only operate as long as they remain neutral, as long as they conduct business to *both* sides. This could get ugly fast!"

"Indeed! The implications are frightening!" J'Sepp rose and paced the room. "But how do you know it is a *third* party? Forgive me, I do not mean to imply that I believe N'Kahv guilty of such treachery, but what evidence do you have to support the theory that another race or faction is responsible? Why could it not be K'Lon, or one of the other Black Market factions?"

"To be honest, I don't have any proof. Just a hunch, a guess. Saying it's K'Lon is too easy. They would naturally fit the bill, but that's exactly why I have a hunch it isn't them. Even though the K'Lonians are an offshoot of N'Kahvians, and they theoretically *could* infiltrate our forces by dyeing their skin pigment from red to green, I believe they are innocent here, for once. I believe it would have to be someone *inside* the N'Kahvian Fleet; someone that would have access to our ships, perhaps a number of people. Who else could commandeer a frigate but one of our allied races? Unless… I must think on this further. For now, go back to your duties and tell no one. Absolutely no one!"

"Yes, Grant, of course," J'Sepp nodded. "Word of this cannot be allowed to spread to the masses. There would be panic, rioting, devastation. Yes, indeed, no one must know! And Grant? I am here should you require my assistance."

"I know, Doc, thanks."

ಬ 5 ೲ

Mason returned to the bridge just as they entered Mak's space. The base was located on a small planetoid no bigger than Sedna in the Sol System. He sat at the conn, which also served as his command chair on such a small ship, and locked in a holding pattern. As he glanced around he noticed that Rhivakkon and Bellatan were not at their posts.

"T'Naan, locate Rhiv and Bell for me, would you?"

"First Officer Bellatan and Operations Officer Rhivakkon are on deck four, crew quarters."

"What are they doing there, Laylaka? Why are you alone up here?"

"Rhiv just needed a moment. I think he is still shocked by what happened. They are alright, though, they are together."

"I keep forgetting how young Rhiv is. He's so good at his job that I forget he's still a child by Myowan terms. He's, what

75, in Myowan years, T'Naan?"

"Correct, Cap, 15 in Terran years if you're curious. This whole experience must be very hard on him. Poor kid... It's his first time offworld and he winds up shot at, kidnapped, and imprisoned."

"Don't go getting soft on me, girl. Hold it together and tell them to get up here, huh?"

"Sure thing, Cap!" Mason could swear there was even a salute in there somewhere. He needed to remember that T'Naan, mature as she sounded, was still only six months out of dry dock, just a baby herself. *What have I gotten my crew into? Raw, untrained, inexperienced... Can we really do this?*

As Bell and Rhiv returned to the bridge, Mason filled them in on his plan. They would search Mak's base, armed of course, for any clue as to what happened or who could have been responsible for his death. Failing in that, they would backtrack Mak's last known course and search for evidence. Ultimately, their own course would take them to Rashal Nalaadi on Phasia 2, one of the most affluent sectors in the galaxy and the headquarters for the Red Moons. Information didn't come cheap, and as information brokers all Red Moons were *very* well off. Mason had never seen Phasia 2, but all the vids showed a paradise. Beautiful landscapes, epic vistas, fantastic shopping, gorgeous beaches, and all the finest handcrafted furnishings the galaxy could provide. It was typically used as a vacationing spot or a hideaway for newly joined couples. Mason had hoped to see it under better circumstances, but *shikata ga nai,* as the Japanese on Terra were known for saying. It cannot be helped.

"Um, Cap! We need to leave, like right now!" T'Naan was panicked, something she *never* was.

"Take control, T'Naan, and explain what's going on. I trust you." Mason and the others swung around in their seats and braced themselves. Within moments T'Naan had cleared the planetoid and achieved escape velocity; something that the bridge crew could not have done as quickly.

"The base! It's exploding!" T'Naan called and the ship strained against the inertia of her rapid escape. No sooner had she spoken, then there was an explosion below and the ship was buffeted by shock waves. The entire planetoid was gone. Only rubble remained.

"Well, change of plans. We will *not* be going down to the base..." Mason said dryly.

The entire crew was gathered in the mess while T'Naan kept watch. Being an A.I. she could be in two places at once, and react at lightning speed. *Must be nice,* Mason thought as he waited for everyone to settle in. *But she is still bound by my commands. Shackled, I guess. Wonder how she feels about that...?*

Once everyone was seated, cups of coffee, tea, or whatever hot beverage his crew ordered, were passed around and quiet fell over the room.

"Mase, what's going on? If this was just a routine

investigation then why did that planetoid just explode?" Bellatan was understandably agitated. Mason was his best friend, they shared everything together, but now Mason was holding out on him, his first officer!

Mason took a sip of his coffee and gagged. "Xhuvina, I think this is yours." He passed her the cup.

"Ah, then this must be yours. Coffee, is it? It tastes horrible!" She crunched up her face and stuck out her tongue.

"I could say the same for that... whatever it is." Mason cringed at the thought of tasting it again. Grainy with a side of tar didn't begin to explain the concoction Xhuvina imbibed with gusto.

"What do you mean? *Heffia* is a delicacy on Tukkol! One of our best and most refreshing beverages!"

"Right. Well, enjoy it. I'll keep my coffee, thanks."

"Go right ahead!" Xhuvina said and took another sip. "It tastes like powdery asphalt to me."

Mason gagged again, but not from the coffee. *Funny, that's exactly what* heffia *tastes like...*

"Stop avoiding my question, Mase." Bell looked even more frustrated. Mason knew he could stall no longer. It was time to tell his crew what was really going on.

"Right, well, you guessed correctly. This mission is not a simple reconnaissance mission. Yes, we are looking into who killed Mak D'Neen, but we are also here to unravel a conspiracy. We think..."

Mason filled in his crew with all the pertinent information. He left out his own suspicions though, and only presented the facts that he and Brantoni had gathered thus far. When he was finished the silence in the room was palpable.

"If anyone wants to pull out now I wouldn't hold it against you, you can even take one of the shuttles back to N'Kahvian space. This could end up being a one-way trip. I understand if you don't want to continue, but I for one will see this thing through. The N'Kahvians took me in when my parents were killed by K'Lonians. I owe them more than I can ever repay. If someone is setting out to destroy my home, then I'm going to fight for it!" Mason waited but no one rose to leave.

Bell looked around the table and said, "We're with you, Captain Mason. All the way." The room resounded with, "Yes, sir!"

Mason was touched by their loyalty and devotion until Laylaka spoke up next.

"Besides," she said with a wink, "Do you know how hard it would be to find another captain this late in the mission?"

ଚ 6 ଓ

They sat around the table in the mess for a few more moments asking questions, hashing out plans, and arguing over strategies, but ultimately they committed themselves to the mission. Their course was set for Phasia 2 and they were less than a day away from Red Moon territory. Mason ordered some down time for his crew because he knew things were going to get tense, and he wanted an alert, agile, and able crew at his disposal. *Besides, T'Naan is capable of running every system simultaneously, in her sleep! Well, if she slept, that is...* Mason thought to himself as he turned from his quarters and entered the lift on deck one.

The T'Naan was a small frigate, only six decks, and not all of them the same size. The Bridge and Captain's Quarters were on Deck One. Deck Two housed the Weapons Arrays and Shields; only two people could successfully move in there at a time with all of the equipment. Deck Three was the Kitchen, Mess Hall, Recreation Rooms and the Gym; the largest deck on the ship. Deck Four was the Crew Quarters, the Medical Bay, and the Science Lab. Deck Five was Engineering and the Engineering Lab, which is also where T'Naan's A.I. core was housed. In addition, it was where the crew could set up a temporary bridge in the event that the main bridge was damaged or destroyed. Lastly, Deck Six contained the Shuttle Bay and Cargo Hold where two basic N'Kahvian shuttles berthed, and also enclosed the bulk of the engine core and propulsion systems, directly below Engineering. In actuality, Engineering was one big deck since there was virtually no separation between them, but it made Mason feel better to say his ship had *six* decks instead of *five*.

The recreation rooms and gym were a little sparse at the moment. Mason was still purchasing the exercise equipment and game tables that he wanted but it was enough for now. Most of his crew was there, watching news vids, or playing *k'chaka*, a N'Kahvian racket game similar to badminton, which Mason loved. Mason didn't want to play today, though. Instead, he turned towards the kitchen to see if Bell was there. He was, and he was preparing something that smelled worse than Mason's birthday cake. Not for the first time Mason regretted his choice of ship's chef. But Bellatan loved being the cook for everyone. Lived for it. He said it gave him a daily opportunity to test a scientific theory. Mason, although it made him feel a little like the vermin that he occasionally found onboard and used for tests, wouldn't take that away from his best friend.

Bell had been through a lot. He lost his wife and three children when K'Lon raided the Ahmbian colony on K'Lendra 4, Kalenandra in the Ahmbian tongue. It was the most brutal and horrific attack in the war, and was almost as devastating as the Uprising. K'Lonian forces cut off supply chains first when they laid siege to the planet. When starvation panic set in among the people, several attempted to leave onboard a science vessel to get help. K'Lonian military apprehended them and brought them down to the surface. They tied each of the crew to a post and let them sit in the harsh sun for one day. Then they found the family members of each person and brought them to the site only to have the crew watch as their loved ones were beaten and left for dead. Yes, the K'Lonians left them there to die! Men, woman, and children, some of them no more than babes! As the crew heard the cries and dying moments of their loved ones they went mad, one by one. The K'Lonians didn't take the bodies away either. The crew not only had to watch, but they had to smell the decomposing bodies of their families. The despair, depression, and anguish along with lack of nourishment killed all eight of them within a few days. But the K'Lonians didn't stop there. They ransacked the colony, burning everything in their wake. Bell was working out in the fields at the time and tried to reach his family. When he arrived home his house was gone, burned to the ground, the door barred from the outside, his family trapped inside. All that was left was his daughter's favorite rag doll which he kept by his bedside.

N'Kahvian troops arrived on K'Lendra 4 as soon as possible, but it was too late, the colony was gone. There is a memorial there now, and K'Lon has made a formal apology for what happened, but no apology could bring back those lost. Bell joined the Imperial N'Kahvian Fleet and vowed to use his knowledge and love of science to assist in any way that he could.

And that led to him meeting Mason and becoming very good friends, and ultimately to him being the ship's chef. *But I really should give him an 'assistant' to 'help' him prepare our meals...* Mason thought as he held his breath upon entering.

"Bell, buddy, what are you making?" Mason tried very hard not to cringe as he took an unsteady breath.

"Spaghetti!" Bell said with obvious glee. "It's your favorite right? I think I have all the ingredients... let's see... baby *alasyn* eels, check... a sauce made from the blood of a *t'larc*, check... herbs and spices, ch – wait, what spices should I use? Would these work? I'll grind them up first, naturally." He held out his hand and inside was a still-moving batch of grubs from who knows where. Mason gagged for the third time that day.

"*Eels*!? And *grubs*!? Bell, are you trying to kill me?!" Mason waved his hand under his nose and pinched up his face.

"Have I done something wrong, Mase?" Bellatan looked stricken as he double-checked his ingredients. "This looks like everything you showed me in the picture..."

"Buddy, spaghetti is made with pasta." At Bell's confused face Mason realized that *none* of the ingredients in spaghetti could be found anywhere in the galaxy. He would never truly taste it again. "Never mind, buddy, I appreciate the effort, really I do, but you can't get the stuff you need anywhere outside of the Sol System, which is lost to us forever."

"Maybe not forever, Mase." Bell patted his shoulder. "The best scientists are still working on it. Don't give up hope."

"It's been 135 years. I'll never get back there. Besides, I don't even really remember it anymore and everyone I ever knew and loved is dead. Terra is no great loss to me."

"Yes, everyone I loved is dead, too... That's why we're such great friends, huh? No love here!" Bell put on a false grin and went back to mixing his ingredients. "No sense letting this all go to waste. If I add a few more ingredients I can make one of my favorite meals, *chilasa*!" He added a few more squirming items to the pot and stirred. Mason didn't like the... *high protein*... diet of Ahmbians and decided to skip this meal.

"Sorry, Bell," he said. "I'll have to pass on dinner this afternoon anyway. I need to work on the details of this mission. I'll just make a sandwich and head back up to the bridge."

"Sure, no problem, Mase," Bell said. "Now, when are you going to tell me what you *really* think this is all about?" He leaned against the counter and crossed his arms. "I figured you didn't want to say in front of the others, but I'm willing to bet you have this thing solved already."

Mason looked over at his long-time friend and went back to fixing his sandwich. "Just a hunch, Bell, just a hunch. Not enough to bank on, yet," he said and turned to leave. "But I'll let you know when I do."

Bell was right. Mason did already have this figured out; he just needed a few more pieces of the puzzle to fall into place first. They were coming up on Phasia 2 and had answered the preliminary hails from the planet below. Now they were awaiting clearance and docking procedures. From way above the planet, Phasia 2 looked just like the pictures and vids from Terra; a big, blue marble with swirling clouds and land masses. Mason couldn't wait to get down there. Just before they left Terra Mason's parents took him on vacation to a place called Florida in North America. Mason loved it! The beach was the best part, but he also enjoyed the rides and games at this *ancient* amusement park that had made Florida famous long ago. Somehow they were able to keep it maintained, but it was mostly a museum. Only a few rides still worked.

As they followed the protocols for docking that the port authorities finally provided, Mason could see that this planet wasn't like Terra at all. The land masses were much smaller and spread out evenly. It almost made it look like his parents chess board but with land and crystal clear water. The closer they got to the main city on the planet the more they could see the high-rise buildings and open pavilions below. They docked high above the surface and took a transit shuttle down to the main shopping district and office complex. Rashal Nalaadi was supposed to be somewhere in this area.

Mason checked over the data on his minicom, a computer database that he wore on his wrist. He had downloaded everything he thought he would need before disembarking. Minicoms also contained all of the medical, financial, and biographical information for the person wearing it and in N'Kahvian space all starship captains and Dauntless military were required to wear one. The rest of the crew had the option to wear one, but most did. K'Lonians banned the technology, but Mason never really understood why. There was so much about the Uprising that didn't make sense to him. Supposedly, the K'Lonians despised the advent of technology and thought that it would be used to control the masses; to take away an individual's freedom and ultimately that it could be used to create a caste system where some would even be denied access to medical aid! Absurd! Mason had seen no evidence of that in the 300 years since the Uprising. All the minicoms were for was to make life a little easier. Banking could be done anywhere, and purchases could be made just by swiping the minicom over a special indicator on most displays and devices. Granted, they were also used to relay his exact position at any given time and upload his recent activities to the central database on N'Kahv, but so what? He didn't have a problem with that and minicoms were exceptionally useful. For example, he used his now to discover what Brantoni knew about Nalaadi. Brantoni found out that Rashal Nalaadi loved to be the tallest person in the room, and would force those taller to kneel or sit in his presence.

There was even a reference to Nalaadi and a custom-made pair of shoes that would elevate his height by five percent! Apparently that gave him an air of superiority and authority. That led Mason to believe he would have the highest office in the tallest building, too.

"Let's start there," he said and pointed. Kotzer, Xhuvina, and Rhiv were with him while the others stayed onboard.

"Why do you believe we should start there, sir?" Kotzer asked.

"Let me guess, Cap," Xhuvina answered, "a hunch?"

"You guessed it!"

They entered through the lobby doors and a holo-display lit up just in front of them. They tried to walk around, but it followed them, hovering just a few feet from their faces.

"*Hello and welcome to Phasia 2, the land of wonders!*" Apparently this thing wasn't going to leave them alone. "*How may I assist you, Captain Mason?*"

"What? How do you know who I am?" Mason asked.

"*When you docked, all of your computer files were uploaded to our database. Standard procedure, I assure you. We do not freely distribute your information; we only use it for security and promotional purposes. However, we cannot be held responsible for what our clients do with your information.*"

How convenient… Mason thought as the display switched to an advertisement for hair spray. The company claimed that by using their product Mason would have the best hair in the galaxy.

Somehow, he doubted that. His auburn mop was always unruly and always would be. The ad continued, *"Yes, even your unruly auburn hair can look this good! Simply swipe your minicom over the indicator now and we will have it delivered to the O.N.S. T'Naan within the hour!"*

"No, thanks," Mason said and tried sidestepping again. Naturally, the display followed them. "Good grief! If this *thing* is going to follow me everywhere then I'm going back to the ship!"

"Oh, come now, Cap!" Xhuvina said. "I'm enjoying all the ads especially suited for Tukkols! Did you see the size of that last one?"

"It was a hair spray ad for Ahmbians. I guess they figured I'd be interested..." Mason replied.

"No, sir. It was a new sleep drug. I find it interesting that it knew I was having trouble sleeping since we started this mission." Kotzer replied.

"Each ad is created solely for the user and directly uploaded to your neural pathways via the BT5000 microchip embedded in your cerebral cortex," the display said.

"Oh now that's *fantastic*!" Mason interjected with clear sarcasm.

"We are so happy that you are pleased! This technology is unique to Phasia 2, but soon manufacturers will release this technology to the highest bidder. Would you like to make an offer?" The display was really getting to Mason now.

"Will you *go away*!?!?" Mason pulled his hand back and

swatted at the display, but since it was a holoprojection his hand went right through instead.

"*If you have a complaint please contact the Customer Service Department at –* "

"Argh!"

"That will be all ALIS," a syrupy voice said behind them. "I apologize for her... overzealousness. She is programmed to greet newcomers to this lobby, but her programming needs work."

"Alice? You named her Alice?" Mason asked the stranger.

"Not Alice as in the name. A-L-I-S. Automated Liaison for Interplanetary Service. ALIS is meant to assist our brokers and stand in as sales representative during peak times. She is just a simple virtual intelligence at the moment, but soon she will be a fully operational A.I. and we shouldn't any more of these... episodes. Now, if you will come with me Captain, Broker Nalaadi is waiting for you upstairs."

"Who are you? And how did you know who I was? Did ALIS tell you?" Mason responded as he followed the gentlemen to the nearest lift.

"I am merely an acolyte of Broker Nalaadi. An apprentice, if you will. My name is not important. Here we are! Good day!" The lift doors opened and all but the stranger stepped out. Another stranger joined them and ushered them into the most luxurious room Mason had ever seen. He hated to admit it but it was grander than the First Kahv's meeting room!

"Broker Nalaadi will be with you in a moment. Please, have a seat. May I offer you refreshments?" The newcomer said.

"No, thank you. We're fine." Mason replied.

The room only offered enormous cushions on the floor that surrounded tables made of pure gold and silver, extremely valuable in this galaxy even though they had become worthless in the Lost Galaxy when he left. Xhuvina plopped down on the nearest one and wiggled around.

"Oooooh, this is nice!" The school girl grin popped out again and Mason just shook his head and chuckled.

"I'm sure ALIS will assist you in getting some for your quarters. Would you like me to call her back?" Mason offered.

"Oh no! Don't do that!" Xhuvina stood up immediately and shook her head frantically. "They aren't *that* great! Those constant ads *were* getting annoying…"

౫ 7 ల

They wandered around the room for a few moments taking in all there was to see. *Nalaadi must be a* very *good broker,* Mason thought. *Everything in this room is quite expensive... So, he likes to show off his wealth, huh? Good to know...* Mason filed it away as a bargaining tool for a later use. They didn't have long to wait, though. A door opened on the other side of the room and a Rusali approached. He wore a long, dark green and blue robe that trailed behind him as he walked. The Red Moons insignia was embroidered on his lapel. His straight dark black hair hung to his waist, typical of Rusali tradition. The men all had long black hair, but the women were all hairless. He also had the typical build of a Rusali male, tall, broad-shouldered, and well-muscled. However, this Rusali also had a bit of a belly. Apparently, he hadn't missed any meals; a strange sight to behold. He went straight to Mason and offered his hand.

"Greetings! I am Rashal Nalaadi. I'm sure you know your lives are in danger and so on and so forth, and your ship is being boarded as we speak, etc., etc., etc. So here is the information you are after and have a wonderful day!" Nalaadi turned and walked back towards the door he just emerged from.

"Wait, *what!?*" Mason asked, flabbergasted. "That's it? Don't we get to talk? What do you mean my ship is being boarded? I haven't heard so much as a peep –" Just then their minicoms all chirped.

"Captain! Please return to the ship. Some men are trying to impound the T'Naan!" Laylaka's voice said over the comm. "Bellatan is trying to hold them off, but they have weapons. This isn't good, Captain. They say we failed to pay the docking tax, the landing party tax, the search tax, the transit shuttle fee, the –"

"I get the idea, Laylaka. They have a lot of fees. I'll be there soon, just stall them!"

"Stall them? Er… right…"

Nalaadi had paused at the door after Mason's exclamation. "Yes, yes, a lot of fees. How do you expect us to operate without fees?"

"We didn't know. There was nothing posted anywhere!" Mason said.

"Why would we *post fees*?" Nalaadi laughed. "Everyone that has ever traveled this galaxy *knows* that Phasia 2 has fees!" Nalaadi continued to laugh hysterically, his round belly jiggling up and down like a *k'ntaka* coming out of hibernation. It would have been comical if the situation wasn't so dire.

"Well, *I* didn't. You seem to have a grasp on our situation, how much do we owe? Who do we pay?"

"Oh, my dear captain. You cannot pay the fees *and* the penalties. You haven't that much money!" Nalaadi continued to laugh and it was really getting to Mason.

"Will you please stop laughing and help us!?" Mason's day just kept getting worse.

"Of course, of course, my dear captain." Nalaadi stopped laughing and walked over to a console. "ALIS, please deduct the fees owed by Captain Grant Mason from my account and pay the necessary parties."

"Certainly, sir," ALIS replied from the console. "Fees deducted, sir. 20 billion *h'ngols*. Shall I send an invoice to Capt. Mason?"

"No, no, that won't be necessary," Nalaadi looked directly at Mason, "this time."

"20... *billion... h'ngols...*" Mason was queasy. He couldn't hope to make that much money in a lifetime, not as a small-time merchant anyway. Maybe if he joined Brantoni in the Black Talons... Nalaadi must be *very* wealthy!

"Never mind the amount; I'll make that up in a day or so." There was a loud plop behind them and Mason turned around. Xhuvina had sat rather heavily on the cushions again. Mason didn't blame her. If he weren't the captain of a starship he would, too!

"Just as long as *you* know…" Nalaadi turned to Mason and somehow he knew, by the look in Nalaadi's violet eyes, that Nalaadi was deadly serious. "You. Owe. Me." With that Nalaadi turned and walked away.

"And I *always* collect a debt."

They returned to the T'Naan and Mason had never been so happy to leave a pleasure planet!

"T'Naan, search the database – as long as there are no *fees*! – for any and all taxes, fees, tariffs, *whatever* that we may encounter on the rest of this mission. I want to know *before* we have to pay them!"

"Aye, Cap!" T'Naan replied. "Requested search will take four days. Do you want to narrow the search?"

"Four days? What are your search parameters?"

"You said any and all, Cap. I'm searching every database on every world in the galaxy, just in case we end up there during this mission."

Mason sighed. He had to remember that she was still a machine; an extremely powerful and well-built machine, with an incredibly lifelike personality, but still a machine. He had to be specific.

"Ok, change parameters. Start with the data we received from Nalaadi. There should be flight paths and locations listed. Search those sites for any taxes and fees that we may encounter should we go to those places. Use your best guess when in doubt or ask me or Bell. What's the ETA on that search?"

"I should have that for you in 40 cycles, Cap."

"Alright, thanks. Get started. Sorry, they boarded you, T'Naan. You okay?"

"Sure Cap, I'm alright. They didn't damage anything. Thanks for asking. Most captains don't even notice or care that the ships get scared when they're boarded…"

"You are a member of my crew, T'Naan, and you were boarded without authorization while I was away. Not only that, they threatened to impound you and who knows what else. That must have been frightening; of course I'm going to check on you. Now, don't go getting soft on me, back to your search."

"Right, Cap!"

Mason went to his quarters to review the data he had received from Nalaadi. He ordered a coffee from Bell, who was in the mess at the moment preparing their fourth and final meal of the day. Within a few moments it was delivered to his quarters and he sat down to study. Mason loved one thing especially about the N'Kahvians; they not only loved coffee but learned the art of growing and brewing it before the Terrans vanished from the galaxy. His parents always had coffee, and when he had his first sip he imagined they were there with him enjoying their own cups. It was really the only connection he had left to his parents, whom he missed greatly at times.

Alright, let's see what we have here… Mason mused. *Wait a minute, this can't be right! If this is true – well, it must be true, the Red Moons* never *give out false information. It's verified and checked a thousand times at least prior to purchase. I had hoped I was wrong about all this... We have to do something! Fast!*

"All hands, to your posts!" Mason ordered over the conn. He raced out of his quarters and onto the bridge. He immediately set course for Brantoni's base on Remin 2 at the fastest speed possible. He *had* to make it in time!

"What's going on, Mase?" Bell asked, still wearing his apron, as the others filed onto the bridge and took up their posts. "I just started cooking."

"We have to get back to Brantoni, fast! Engineering, can you give me any more power?"

"Not for long, Cap. I can boost the flow of antiprotons to the power core, but we can't sustain it for long. I can give you... 30 cycles, max!"

"Do it!" Mason ordered.

ജ 8 ౪

As they arrived at Remin 2 there was already a battle in progress. Talon ships were fighting not only N'Kahvian ships, but K'Lonian as well. Mason sent the T'Naan behind one of the planet's six moons hoping to mask their energy signature.

"Bell, you're in command. I'm going down there. Keep this ship hidden! J'Sepp," Mason called over the comm. "You're with me. Meet me in the shuttle bay."

"Captain," Laylaka said, "You cannot go down there right now! What if the fight is worse down there?"

"I *know* it is!" Mason called and stepped into the lift.

J'Sepp met him in the shuttle bay with his medical kit and handed him a standard issue pulse disperser. Mason wished he had one of those fancy magnatomic particle dispersers instead. He was certain he was going to need it.

"This is going to get bad, J'Sepp, real bad. If I'm right,

and I'm pretty sure I am, we're going to need your knowledge down there."

"Of course, Grant," J'Sepp replied. "I am always ready."

They skipped the pre-launch sequence and quickly went down to the planet. It was night on Brantoni's side of the planet, and Mason chose a dark and secluded spot to land, but it meant they would have to walk at least half a mile to reach Brantoni. *No choice*, Mason thought. *We need to stay hidden as long as possible*. They moved as quickly and quietly as they could but progress was just too slow.

"Ok, Doc," Mason said. "Can you keep up with me if I run?"

"I don't think that will be a problem, Grant." J'Sepp dropped to his four arms and scuttled along faster than Grant could imagine. "Are you coming, Captain?"

Mason just shook his head and smiled. His adopted people never ceased to amaze him. In his 30 years with the N'Kahvians, he never knew they could do that! How had he *never* seen it before? He hustled to keep up.

They arrived at Brantoni's base only to find it completely destroyed. A search of the nearby buildings yielded no results either. Where was Brantoni? He *had* to find him!

Suddenly he and J'Sepp were grabbed from behind and taken into an alleyway.

"Why are you here?" Brantoni asked. "Have you come back to kill me, too?" He pulled a disperser and pointed it straight between Mason's eyes.

"No, actually," Mason pushed the disperser aside. "I've come to get you out of here!"

"I'm not leaving! Not until that no account brother of mine is dead!" Brantoni spat on the ground. "You're either with me or against me. Make your choice, Captain Mason."

"I guess I'm with you, for now," Mason replied. "Where are you hiding out? We need to talk."

"This way. There are only a few left that I can trust. It was a coup! A bloody coup! By my own brothers, too. Can you believe that?"

"It's worse than that actually; you are just a small part of it all. No offense."

"You mean this day gets worse?" Brantoni stopped and looked at Mason aghast. "I'm about to be killed in cold blood by my own brothers, and you tell me that's insignificant? Geez, man! I mean, c'mon!"

"Sorry, but it's true. Let's get somewhere safe and I'll fill you in."

"There's nowhere left on this planet that's safe. I just have one more brother to kill and we can be off of it. Tommy-boy went down easy, but he was always a softie, now I just have to find Georgie-boy. I know he's around here somewhere's."

"Correct, Mikey," a voice said behind them. "And now to finish you off. Turn around, slowly. I'm a lot of things, but I would never kill my own brother when his back is turned. Anyone else, yeah sure, but not my own brother. We're family, after all."

They turned around and Mason met the only other Terran left in the galaxy. Well, maybe. His day was just full of surprises. They were greeted by at least ten other men all pointing weapons of various sizes and shapes at them.

"Ah, Captain Mason," George Brantoni said, "You were supposed to be killed on Mak's base when we blew it up. Very inconvenient of you not to be there. That was just rude."

"My apologies." Mason replied.

"And you somehow managed to get off of Phasia 2. Even after we bribed the port authorities to hold your ship. You're making it extremely difficult to kill you, you know."

"I was going for 'impossible' actually. Guess I'll have to try harder next time."

George Brantoni backhanded Mason and several guards held him down.

"Now, on to you, brother. Do you know why all this is happening?"

"No, I wish I did," Mike Brantoni said. "Care to enlighten me?"

"Not really. Let's go." They were ushered to a shuttle and tied to a post. The shuttle lifted off and Mason had no idea how they were going to get out of this one. *Think, Mase, think!*

The shuttle docked inside the bay of an enormous K'Lonian warship, *m'nthala* class. Sixty decks, fifteen shuttles, five heavy cruisers, five hundred fighters, and manned by two thousand of the most elite troops the K'Lonians possessed. *There are only ten ships like this in existence! How did it get here without anyone knowing it? And how does it factor into all this?* Mason thought as they were shoved down the corridors and into the lift. They were... deposited, to put it mildly... in a cell in the ship's brig.

"Mason, care to tell me what's going on and how the heck we're going to get out of this?" Brantoni asked.

"Gimme a moment," Mason replied. He tapped a spot just behind his left ear, a homing device that linked to his BT5000 and transmitted his coordinates to T'Naan and the supercomputer on N'Khav. He hoped someone would be able to receive the signal through this incredibly powerful and possibly well-shielded warship. He had the device implanted by J'Sepp soon after taking command of the T'Naan. Something told him it would come in handy someday, perhaps that day was today.

"Okay, so here's what's happening. This isn't just about the Black Talons. This coup is against *all three powers in this galaxy*! It's a joint effort between the N'Kahvians, the K'Lonians and the Conglomerate. But not the governments, it's the people. There has been an underground movement to end this 300 year stalemate for a long time, and now they finally have the resources they need to do it. They have weapons and technology from the Talons, they have –"

"Wait a minute; I never supplied no underground before. What are you talking about?" Brantoni asked.

"You didn't, but your brothers did. They kept you in the dark. Probably because they figured you would be against it."

"You bet I would! I make a lot of money through this arrangement. There's no way I would undermine the Accord!"

"Precisely! This war has become about money and who has the biggest toys. Does anyone even remember *why* they are fighting? What's this war about? Can you answer?"

"Yeah, it's about... uh... well..." Brantoni couldn't answer the question after all.

"I will educate you on the basis of this war." J'Sepp said. "The Uprising came about because a group of people did not want all of the technology and advances brought by the Terrans. Yes, it was a new day for N'Kahv, but not everyone appreciated the ability to travel the stars and meet new races. They were xenophobic. They believed that mixing with other races would pollute the purity of the N'Kahvian blood lines and we would lose our identity as a people. They also believed that this new technological age would destroy the socioeconomic stability of N'Kahv. They were afraid that those in power would use technology as a weapon of sorts to subjugate the people, to deny them the basic necessities of life, to elevate some and oppress others.

"As time passed this group became larger and larger. In an effort to find a peaceful solution First Kahv E'Tyen, my grandfather, proposed that the group find a new homeworld where they would be free to live as they chose. He even sent people out on survey missions to find a suitable planet for them. There was only one in the galaxy that was nearly identical to N'Kahv, K'Lon. His plan backfired, however. The people believed that the First Kahv wanted to eliminate them. That he would destroy the ships as they left orbit or that the planet was inhospitable to N'Kahvian life. Fights erupted all across N'Kahv. It was devastating. Finally, my grandfather had no choice. He found as many rebels as he could and forced them to leave.

"Never before in the history of N'Kahv has such a time existed. The First Kahv was an inherited position, passed on from one generation to the next. But if the people had no confidence in the new First Kahv, he could be replaced by another member of the royal family and the line would continue through that First Kahv. The people decided based on the principles and integrity of the new First Kahv, and if he was agreeable to them they supported him with their entire being. There had never been such division among the people before. Nor had there ever been a time when the First Kahv was rejected by the people.

"The ships made it safely to K'Lon and they discovered that the First Kahv had their best interests at heart after all. But that did not stop them from hating him or N'Kahv for forcing them from their homes, their friends, and even their families. They used the ships that brought them to K'Lon to travel back to N'Kahv where they assassinated my grandfather and burned all of the government buildings, museums, cultural centers, and temples to the ground. It was devastating. I cannot recall a time when I have seen more suffering."

"Wait, you were there? That was 300 years ago!" Brantoni said.

"Yes, I was there. N'Kahvians are not as long lived as the Myowans, but we can live for about three hundred years. I am very old, three hundred and ten to be precise, nearing the end of my life. I assume this is the reason you brought me along, Grant, the knowledge you spoke of? To tell the history as one of the oldest living N'Kahvians left who *remembers* it?"

"Yes, it is. Thank you for understanding. I had no choice but to put you in harm's way in order to expose this conspiracy. Please continue, there is more to the story, isn't there?"

"Indeed. After the Uprising, the time I spoke of, the rebels left N'Kahv permanently. They invited anyone who wanted to join them and 'live free' as they called it to meet them at the ships the following week. They even used the technology on N'Kahv to change their pigments to red so that they were truly no longer N'Kahvians. They called themselves K'Lonians, after their new homeworld, and several hundred thousand N'Kahvians joined them as well as many other races. They set up a system of government for themselves as well, and closed the borders of their world. Those of us that remained put the pieces of our lives back together the best we could. I was the only remaining member of the royal family and thus the title of First Kahv fell to me. The people deplored the idea of a ten year old First Kahv and overthrew the government. That is why the First Kahv is now an elected position, renewed every ten years, but we still keep the names of our ancestors; Imperial, First Kahv, etc., though we are now truly a republic. Ah, those were dark times. Dark times indeed."

"I'm still a little confused…," Brantoni said. "How does all this figure into the back-and-forth war that we're all stuck in now? If the K'Lonians closed their borders and denied technology, how come they order weapons and tech from me?"

"Remember that system of government they set up?" Mason said. At Brantoni's nod he continued, "Well, they set up a dictatorship inadvertently. They called it the Republic of Free K'Lon. Free from technology and all its advances. Free to live as they had on N'Kahv before the Terrans showed up. They wanted to do away with the people having total control over their governmental leadership since that's what allowed the Terrans to land on N'Kahv and bring their technology with them. They believed that those kinds of decisions shouldn't be left up to the masses, who probably didn't truly understand the ramifications of such actions. They set up a leader, D'Viak Prime after the N'Kahvian word for freedom, but granted him power to overthrow any decision by the people that he or she believed would ultimately destroy them. Well, I don't have to tell you how fast that went bad, do I? The people only held one election. One. That leader seized control and held it until he died about thirty years ago. His son inherited the position and he is just as lethal as his father. They both continued the war needlessly. N'Kahv granted them sovereignty over their planet, established them as a completely separate entity, and even provided them with all the things they would need to make a home on K'Lon, but the D'Viak Prime wanted more. He wanted to completely dominate the galaxy, not share it. He sought the complete and total annihilation of N'Kahv and all the people on it or scattered throughout the galaxy. He reluctantly entered into agreements for the Accord, set up shortly after things quieted down from the Uprising, and bided his time until he had acquired enough resources to continue the fighting that started on N'Kahv. That's when this current war started and it's simply one man's grab for power. Over time we have lost sight of the real reason we are fighting, the thing that started this war. N'Kahv was protecting itself from a madman. Now it has become a series of retaliations, they retaliate for something we are retaliating for.

"So, how do the Talons fit into all this?"

"You supplied the weapons and tech that K'Lonians couldn't begin to make for themselves, and you still provide it for them. Remember when I said there was an underground movement? Well, the people of K'Lon are desperate to get out from under a dictator. They have, over the past three hundred years, built a network, a community, to break free and live as they choose, but the D'Viak Prime has complete dominance over their planet, nothing is bought or sold without his people knowing about it. The K'Lonian people are starving; they lack medicine and the basic necessities for life.

"I just discovered this recently. Before now I believed the propaganda, that they were still angry over the Uprising and still wanted a fight. It simply isn't true. Somehow, word spread throughout the galaxy that the K'Lonians wanted freedom and an end to the war but had no means to fight back against the D'Viak Prime. Other races, N'Kahvians, Myowans, Rusali, Ahmbians, Nipoli, Tukkols, they all joined in to free K'Lon, but in order for that to happen they needed to get the three biggest powers to fall. As long as there was an Accord among the leadership there was no way the people could win. Your brothers supplied the weapons and ships for the underground, free of charge. That's why you noticed so many missing shipments. My guess was that they were diverted somewhere and they were, to the underground. The Silver Daggers have been sent to infiltrate and assassinate the leaders of each faction, including their own. Only those that are a part of the underground, such as your brothers, would be spared. The Red Moons in the underground, I'm assuming Nalaadi is one of them, controlled the information that got out and hid anything to do with their plans. Now it's up to us to expose this thing to the galaxy. We have to get out of here first, though…"

ೞ 9 ಚ

Mason stood up and approached the entrance to the cell. A forcefield was in place, he could hear the hum from where he was standing and had no intentions of finding out how strong it was. Just then a door opened and George Brantoni stepped onto the brig.

"Now that you understand everything, it's time to kill you. I can't take the chance that you will interfere, especially now that you know we denied you billions of *h'ngols* in profits." He lowered the forcefield and that's when J'Sepp vaulted. He held George fast, using all six limbs.

"Go! Now! I cannot contain him for long!"

"Not without you! Where's his disperser?" Mason looked around, but Brantoni beat him to it.

"Count of three, you release and I shoot him! One, two, th—"

He was cut off as guards came rushing onto the brig, weapons firing. J'Sepp threw George Brantoni into the brig just as Mason turned on the field. The crackling and sizzling could be heard throughout the deck.

"Good riddance," Mike Brantoni said as they dodged weapons fire.

"You're happy about this?" Mason was incredulous. "After what we just told you?"

"You heard him," Brantoni replied as he ducked behind a console and fired using his brother's disperser. "He said *billions*! I want my money! I don't care about their stupid fight!"

Mason just sighed and pried lose a grate at the back of the room. He crawled inside. It looked like the maintenance tubes on his ship. He hoped so because they had no other options at the moment. "In here! I think this will take us to the shuttle bay!" They followed him in, Brantoni taking up the rear and laying down cover fire.

Just then the ship rocked with powerful explosions. Something was going on outside and Mason had a hunch that the reinforcements had arrived.

"What was that?" Brantoni asked.

"Just hurry! I think it's through here."

"How can you tell?" Brantoni inquired.

"I kept track of how many turns we took and how many levels down we went, how else?" Mason looked at Brantoni askance.

"Oh, naturally."

They exited right where they should, the shuttle bay. Commandeering a shuttle on the other hand, would prove difficult. There were hundreds of people in the bay, all prepping to launch the fighters and cruisers. It was mass pandemonium.

Mason knocked out a passing guard and took his weapon and clothing. Brantoni did the same. Mason was glad the guards all wore helmets; it would be easier to conceal their faces that way. J'Sepp on the other hand...

"Ok, here's what we will do," Mason started.

"No, here is what I will do." J'Sepp ran out on all six and pulled the attention of the immediate area. Brantoni rushed towards the closest shuttle. Mason was torn, should he go after J'Sepp or follow Brantoni?

"Go!" J'Sepp yelled in N'Kahvian. "Don't make this all for nothing!"

Mason followed Brantoni, but he promised himself he was not leaving J'Sepp behind. Upon entering the shuttle he discovered Brantoni at the conn rapidly punching in commands.

"I know this warship, I designed it. If they haven't changed the command codes... Ha! They haven't! Now to just..." The lights went out in the shuttle bay and the bay doors started to open.

"J'Sepp is out there! He'll be sucked into space! Close the doors!" Mason started punching buttons until he felt Brantoni's disperser against the side of his head.

"I'm getting out of here, you do what you want, but *don't interfere*!"

"Excuse me gentleman, but are we leaving or staying? I should like to know before they restore power."

Both Terrans turned around and there was a N'Kahvian that looked shockingly like J'Sepp sitting in the back all strapped in, the shuttle sealed tightly behind him.

"J'Sepp?" Mason asked.

"Yes, of course, Grant," J'Sepp responded. "You didn't think I planned to *die* out there, did you?"

They returned to the T'Naan, or rather where the T'Naan *should* have been…

"Computer, ship-to-ship." Mason waited for the chirp, but there was nothing. "Computer?"

Brantoni laughed. "This ship was designed for K'Lonians, Mason. No A.I. allowed."

Mason felt like an idiot. It was only then that he saw the markings inside the ship. All K'Lonian. He tapped a few keys and spoke again.

"Captain Mason to the O.N.S. T'Naan. T'Naan, where are you?"

"Mase! We thought you were still onboard the warship! Where are ya buddy?" Bell's unmistakable voice came over the comm.

"We're where you *should* be. Come pick us up, would ya?

I'm getting hungry for supper."

"Sure thing, Mase! Did you see? I ordered reinforcements. T'Naan broadcast your conversation on all the common channels. The whole galaxy heard the story! The First Kahv ordered an immediate rescue operation to get you and J'Sepp out of there and back on the homeworld. He has also communicated to the underground that he will offer the aid of the entire Imperial N'Kahvian Fleet to help free K'Lon."

"That's great! T'Naan, excellent work! Remind me to treat you to something special when we get back. You've earned it!"

"Sure thing, Cap! I thought that you'd be happy with my decision." He could picture T'Naan grinning from ear to ear. *If she had ears, that is... Port to starboard? Fore to aft?* Mason couldn't tell.

"We should be all finished here, right Cap?" Bell came back over the comm.

The T'Naan was just coming into view. Mason saw a quick flash of light from somewhere behind the T'Naan. As he watched it grew bigger and bigger until it was right on top of them. *What is that...?*

"Bell! Incoming! T'Naan!" Mason screamed over the comm. Their shields were lowered to take on the shuttle; there was no way to avoid the incoming magnatomic plasma wave. *Without shields...* "T'NAAN!!!"

Mason boarded the T'Naan as fast as he could. He shook as he saw the debris, fires, and destruction that the wave caused. It was banned technology because it had the power to completely destroy a world. The wave should have completely disintegrated the ship, pulled it apart atom by atom. It was a miracle that T'Naan heard him and brought the shields back online in time. But she was a good ship, she saved her crew.

"T'Naan, good job," Mason said. Silence. "T'Naan? Are you there, girl?" No response.

Mason climbed over tubing and cables, skirted around fires and worked his way down to the A.I. core. Burned out. Completely. It would be impossible to replace all the damaged circuitry.

"Oh, T'Naan." Mason rested his head against the A.I. core casing and cried. He felt like he had lost a dear friend. An irreplaceable part of himself.

"Cap? Is that you?" T'Naan's small and shaky voice came over the comm.

"T'Naan! You didn't answer... Are you alright?"

"I hurt, Cap... Bad... I hurt bad, Cap... Cap?" She started to whimper and the fear in her voice was crushing to Mason.

"We're gonna fix you up, girl, just hold on."

"Cap? I'm scared. Am I going to die? It hurts bad, Cap, and it's getting so dark. So dark and cold..."

"You fight T'Naan! Hang on, we're gonna fix you up, just hang on. I won't leave you, T'Naan. I'll stay right here."

"Promise?"

"I promise."

Mason used the communications array on the pilfered shuttle to call one of the N'Kahvian warships for a tow. They took the T'Naan onboard, but even the best engineers would have a very hard time putting her back together. Mason was devastated. He loved that ship. He loved T'Naan. She was like a sister to him and a very dear friend. She deserved better than to be shot in the back. They just had to save her, they had to!

"Hey Cap," Xhuvina said. Mason could tell she had been crying, they all had. Each and every person in his crew loved T'Naan, and knowing she sacrificed herself for them – she had provided extra shielding around the bridge and engineering, but it cost her the shielding around her A.I. core – made everyone feel the loss a little bit deeper.

"Hey," Mason responded. "I'm okay. Really I am."

"Right. I'm a Tukkol and I'm crying like a baby. You're just a squishy Terran, you should be a puddle."

Mason smiled at her obvious attempt to cheer him up. They sat together for a long time and relived missions of the past and the crazy little things T'Naan did to make their days brighter.

"This has been one long and lousy day, Xhuvina," Mason said. "It started with a catastrophe in the power core, which was just a ruse to get me to go to a horrible birthday party. Then we get shot at, captured, and imprisoned, all before lunch! To make matters worse, we get nearly blown up, fined out the rear by Phasia 2, captured again, imprisoned again, and I lose the best ship a captain could hope for. This has definitely been the longest 36-hour day in N'Kahvian history."

"Still got one more hour left of the day, Cap. It could get worse."

"I have no doubt."

The lead engineer reported that the T'Naan couldn't be saved. They tried to at least save her computer matrix, but they were too late. She was gone. *Yep,* Mason thought. *It got worse. Oh T'Naan… I'm so sorry… I let you down.*

ಖ 10 ಬ

The fighting would continue for a very long time, it wasn't easy to overthrow a regime, but Mason ordered the crew to report back to N'Kahv for some much needed rest. He needed to see about getting a new ship, too. He decided he just wanted a virtual intelligence this time, no A.I. to love and lose. To his surprise everyone wanted to be a part of his next mission, if he went back out, that is. They said they had never served a better or more devoted captain and desired to stay on with him if he would have them. He was touched beyond words and it helped the sting of losing T'Naan a little. Even so, he grieved.

Half a year later the crew was together again. The fighting to liberate K'Lon was progressing albeit slowly. With the entire N'Kahvian Fleet at their disposal the freedom fighters had all the support they needed, but the D'Viak Prime was very strong and had been controlling the flow of information, technology, and weapons for a very long time. Mason knew this war was going to last awhile.

They were all gathered in the mess hall aboard Mason's new ship after J'Sepp's and Mason's ceremony. They had been awarded the Imperial Star, the highest honor in N'Kahvian society and awarded to those that displayed incredible patriotism and courage in the line of duty. Both military and civilian alike could receive this award and to Mason's knowledge, it had only been given five times in the last one hundred years. Mason was honored to even be considered for the award since technically he isn't N'Kahvian, but the First Kahv merely laughed and said he was the most nonsensical N'Kahvian he had ever met. Then he awarded him the Star and extended his duties to also include Dauntless reconnaissance missions and Morning Light diplomacy missions. Mason was touched. He really did belong to these people, not just in word, but in deed as well.

Now they were commissioning his new ship. It felt strange to be on a ship so soon after losing T'Naan. It had always taken a year or more to get a new ship, he could never afford it, but the First Kahv insisted on providing one for him as soon as possible. This ship was different but similar, too. It was the same basic design, but the Captain's Quarters were on Deck Four with the other crew. That made the Bridge much larger and now the weapons and shields could be operated there, too.

Also, there was no A.I. on this ship, so there was no need for an A.I. core. Mason couldn't bring himself to captain another

A.I. controlled ship. He never really understood how an A.I. felt before T'Naan. He never paid any attention at all really. But T'Naan was *alive*. She was vibrant and witty and devoted. And gone. He just couldn't go through that again. Thus, his new ship only had a rudimentary computer. No A.I. It could communicate – it had a voice – but no personality. No awareness. No life. *And that means no life to lose either,* Mason thought.

"Well," Mason said, "we need a name for this ship. Any ideas?"

"I have one." The doors swished open and a woman walked in to the mess hall.

"Yes? And you are..." Mason had his back to her and when he turned around to face the newcomer he was shocked. She was beautiful, but the most interesting thing about her was that she was Terran! Mason didn't think it was possible to be surprised anymore, but he was wrong.

The woman stared at him with a slow smile on her face. "Don't you recognize me?" She asked in a sultry voice.

"No, I'm afraid we have never met before, Miss...?" Mason replied. Her voice sounded familiar, but he couldn't place her. He looked around the room to see if anyone else recognized her, but they all shook their heads.

"Come now, Cap," the woman said. "It's me, T'Naan!"

Mason gasped. Now he recognized that voice! "But – but – but how? You were destroyed! When? What? T'Naan!" He hurried over to her and stopped midstride. "Are you really

T'Naan?"

"It's really me, Cap," T'Naan said. She walked, no more like sashayed, over to the nearest table and sat down. She crossed her legs in the most seductive way Mason had ever seen. Bell came up and tapped his chin. Apparently Mason's jaw dropped.

"The ship you knew as T'Naan is gone, that's true," T'Naan started. "But when I realized I couldn't be saved I used the last of my reserves and uploaded my entire matrix to the central computer on N'Kahv. The upload completed just in time, too. The old A.I. core died just moments after. It took some doing, but I was able to access the First Kahv's private minicom. He listened to my story and immediately commissioned a team of engineers to build me this new body! They even let me decide how I should look! Do you like it?"

All Mason could do was nod. Bell put both hands on the sides of Mason's head. Apparently Mason hadn't stopped nodding.

T'Naan walked to his side and grabbed his arm. "I can do all of the same things I used to do, but it's significantly slower now. Well, unless I link to this new ship. Xhuvina?" T'Naan turned to the engineer and asked, "Is there an A.I. core on this ship? I looked on Deck Five, but I couldn't find it."

"No, there isn't," Xhuvina replied. "I'm sure the captain can have one installed though, right, Cap?"

"Uh...uh... right," Mason stammered. He was staring down at T'Naan wearing a skin-tight green jumpsuit. Her brunette hair hung to her shoulders with just the slightest wave to it. Her blue eyes were piercing and so deep that he could get lost in them. The corners of her mouth turned up just a little, and when she smiled the world lit up. "We can have that installed right away. It's so great to have you back, T'Naan!"

"So, you're happy, Cap?" T'Naan asked with a smile.

"I sure am! I thought you were gone forever. I felt like I lost part of myself. Now you're back and better than ever! You can go on away missions with us, too, or pick up deliveries, go on science surveys, whatever you want now that you have mobility. Just ask and it's yours." The rest of the crew chimed in with their agreement as well, and laughed over Mason's giddiness.

"That sounds wonderful!" T'Naan said and flashed everyone her best smile. She held Mason's arm just a little bit tighter and leaned against him, but Mason didn't mind at all.

Laylaka's glare could melt all the ice on Haribon 3…

ଧ Epilogue ଔ

Mason returned to his quarters after the celebration and commissioning of the new T'Naan. He had submitted a work order for a blank A.I. core as well, so that T'Naan could interface with this new ship. As he lay on his bed and thought about how wonderful it was to have T'Naan back, his minicom chirped. He tapped a button and a message flared to life in a holo-display:

> *Captain Mason:*
>
> *So glad you like your new ship's avatar. I was happy to provide the funds for her. Just remember, I always collect a debt.*
>
> > *Sincerely yours,*
> >
> > *Rashal Nalaadi*

TO BE CONTINUED

CAPTAIN GRANT MASON

Vs

THE SUPERNOVA

Turn the page for a sneak peek!

Mason ran as fast as he could down to the mess hall once the lift doors opened, but he was too late.

"I WILL NOT!" H'Eyli screamed with a loud crash. As he opened the door to the mess hall he narrowly avoided being decked by a flying spatula. H'Eyli was picking up various objects and hurling them around the mess.

"I will not take orders from you! You can't even smell! How can you possibly cook?!? I am head chef now!" She threw another pot in Bell's general direction. She had grown to about 185 centimeters now and was glowing a bright blueish white. If Mason didn't calm her down fast the ship's automatic fire suppression system would click on and that would just make her angrier.

"Haley, calm down," Mason said, "I can exp –"

"IT'S H'EYLI, YOU WORTHLESS EXCUSE FOR A CAPTAIN!" She glowed brighter and the pan in her hands started to melt.

"Ahh! I'm sorry, I'm sorry!" Mason just couldn't win. Women just plain hated him, that's all there was to it. Had to be.

He tried again, "Hay-lee, right? I'm sorry about that, I am unfamiliar with the Nipoli naming structure. Or is it B'Rai? Anyway, you are here as an assistant to Bellatan, not the head chef. There must have been some error when they informed you of my request. If you prefer to remain on the station that can be arranged, but if you are going to stay on this ship you will take orders from Bell. Understood?" Mason stood straighter and tried to wear the air of authority.

H'Eyli thundered up to him and glared down. "FINE!" She turned and set the melted pan down on the counter. It stuck firm as it cooled. They would never be able to remove it now. Slowly, she turned and walked out of the mess. Mason noticed that she returned to what he assumed was her normal size as she moved. By the time she reached the mess doors she was back to 145 centimeters. Astounding.

"Mase, buddy," Bell said as he crawled out from under one of the work tables, "what have you done now, huh?"

About the Author:

Rebecca M. Norris is many things, an author is just one of them. She became a Christian at age nine and loves sharing Jesus with those around her. She has traveled to South Korea where she spent time as a university English professor at Korea Nazarene University, and also where she met a man that shared the same loves she did including a secret desire for a *Lord of the Rings* themed wedding. She married him, of course! She is now the proud wife of a terrific man who cheers her on no matter what she chooses to undertake. She is also the mother of two beautiful daughters who make her laugh and challenge her at the same time. Mostly, Rebecca M. Norris is just your average woman who loves life and the people she shares it with, including you, her readers!

Visit her at rebeccanorrisbooks.com!

By Scott Norris

Scott Norris is a fantasy and satire author who lives in Kansas City with his wife and two daughters.

Visit Scott at: www.scott-norris.com and scottnorriswrites.medium.com

The Chronicles of Solatia
Book One: Marno's Shield

In the country of Syren, young boys are becoming men in the time-honored tradition of the Age of Ascension Ceremony. Upon the conclusion of the ceremony, the King of Syren and the King of Maif sign a lasting treaty of peace. Marno, who just passed his Ascension, believes his future is bright.

Then a betrayal of epic proportions throws his world into chaos. Marno and his best friend, Tigrand, must sacrifice everything in a war they are ill prepared for… or lose it all forever.

Coming Soon!

The Coronavirus Bible:
Revised Satirical Version

by John Spencer, David S Smith, **Scott Norris**, Paul Kerensa, Michael Richard Bullock, Nathan Ramsden-Lock, Israel Matthews, Pete Hawkins, Toby Isaacson, David Regier

The Coronavirus Bible is what happens when a bunch of Christian Comedians get together (virtually) during quarantine to raise money to support those in need. This Coronavirus Comedy Bible will not only raise a laugh but also raise funds to help those in need with all proceeds from this book going to charity.

The Best of the Salty Cee
COVID Edition: Christian News Satire

by John Spencer, **Scott Norris**, Richie Richards

The Salty Cee is an online Christian News Satire
website that doesn't take itself too seriously. This
special coronavirus survival edition contains another
50 of their best COVID satirical articles that poke fun
at Christian culture and celebrities.

The Best of the Salty Cee
Vol. 2: Christian News Satire

by John Spencer, Nick Angelis, **Scott Norris**

The Salty Cee is an online Christian News Satire
website that doesn't take itself too seriously. This
second volume contains another batch of more than
40 of their best-loved articles that poke fun at
Christian culture and celebrities.

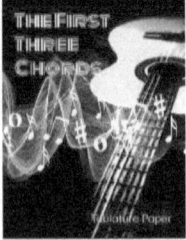

Made in the U.S.A.

Duskraven Entertainment, LLC

P.O. Box 3795
Olathe, KS 66063

ISBN 9798985097108

9 798985 097108